My Glasses

Sponsored by:

Capital BlueCross
1-800-KIDS-101

A publication of the American Literacy Corporation for Young Readers
Reinforced for library use

Text copyright © 2010 by Floyd Stokes.
Illustrations copyright © 2010 by Sheena Hisiro.
Graphic design by Sheena Hisiro.
First Edition, 2011. All rights reserved.

ISBN 978-0-9832490-0-9

PRINTED IN CHINA

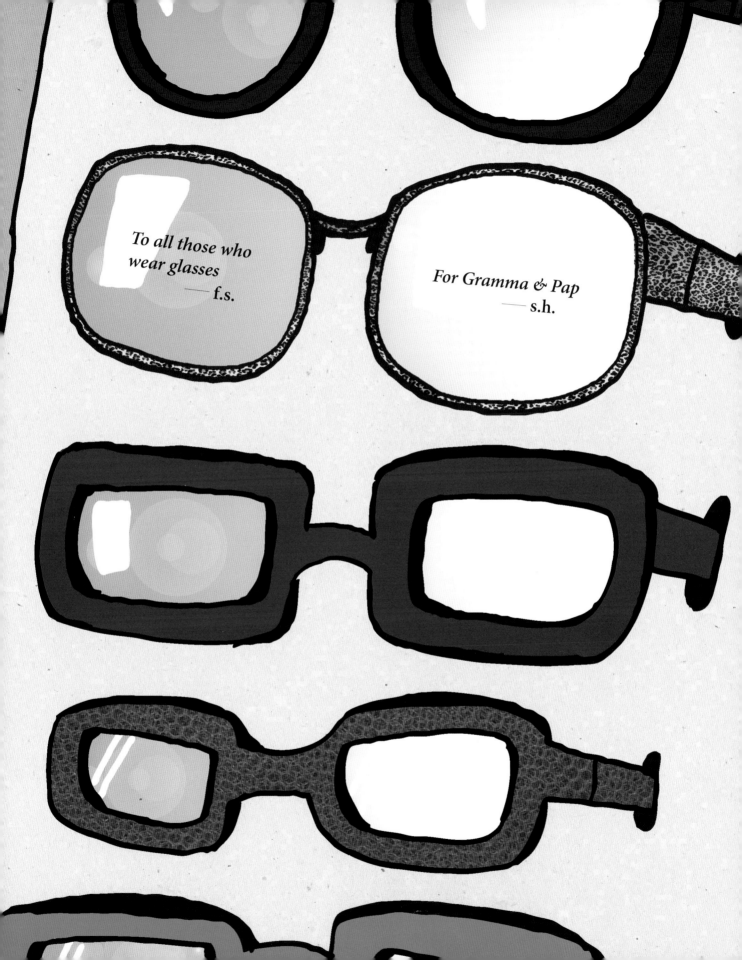

To all those who
wear glasses
—— f.s.

For Gramma & Pap
—— s.h.

My Glasses

written by
Floyd Stokes

illustrated by
Sheena Hisiro

When reading

studying

and at play

They help me see things far and near

They help me see things very clear

Eagles can see farther than any other animal and can spot a hare at about 2 miles away.

I didn't want to wear them at first

Human eyes blink about 22 times a minute.

But my vision kept getting worse

A human eyeball weighs about one ounce.

MY EYES

I went to the doctor to take a test

He took his time, he was the best

Snellen Chart

Jumping spiders have four pairs of eyes that can see 360 degrees around them.

I tried reading the letters from a to d but I needed glasses to help me see

Picking out glasses was a lot of fun

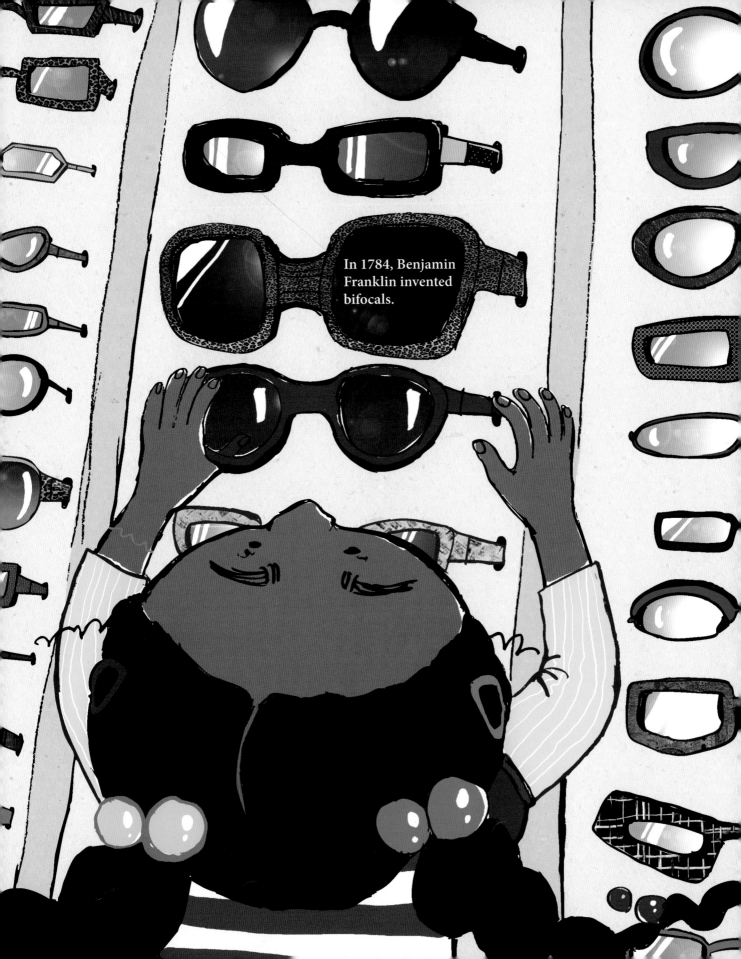

In 1784, Benjamin Franklin invented bifocals.

They even had ones I could wear in the sun

In 1929, sunglasses were invented by Sam Foster.

Some glasses can protect your eyes

Wearing them during sports is very wise

In 1508, Leonardo da Vinci described and sketched the first ideas for contact lenses.

There are so many glasses from
which to choose

Some are red, some are blue

some are *fancy*

The colossal squid's eyeballs are the largest at about 12 inches each.

Glasses Care

some are plain

some are *different*

some are the same

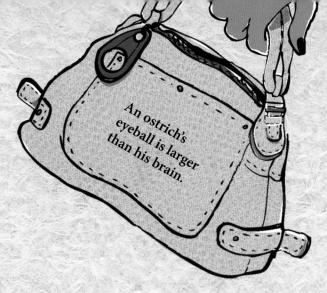

An ostrich's eyeball is larger than his brain.

In the end I picked a pair
That I wasn't ashamed to wear

And held my head up in the air

Around 1284, Salvino D'Armate invented the first wearable eyeglasses.

THE BOY WHO CRIED WOLF

I wear them at home and at school

Floyd Stokes is the founder and executive director of the American Literacy Corporation (ALC). He has written five books: *Teddy, The Hungry Little Bear, Say Ahh! The Teeth Book, Popcorn, There Was an Old Lady Who Lived in a Shoe* and *The Boy Who Cried Wolf!*. On May 1, 2009, he was awarded an honorary doctorate of humanities from Central Penn College. In 2010, he read to children in all 50 states.

For more info, visit:
www.superreader.org

Sheena Hisiro has been drawing since she could hold a pencil. She currently lives in Brooklyn, where she is still drawing and loving every minute of it. Sheena has a BFA in Communications Design from Pratt Institute.

For more info, visit:
oodlesofdoodles.tumblr.com